BAYOU MICROBE IS A WORK OF FICTION.

Any references to historical events, real people, or real places are used factiously. Names, characters, places, and events are products of the author's imagination, and resemblance to actual events or places or persons, living or dead, is entirely coincidental.

Bayou Microbe

a novelette

by

Janet Goodrich

Published by depict books.

ISBN 978-0-9900037-5-5

depict books
13714 Briarlake Avenue
Baton Rouge, LA 70809

Armand and Celeste LeDay's centuries old lifestyle is destroyed by an invasion of globs of oil from a spill and their environment is infected by its saviors. The marshland is saturated with oil-eating microbes and when they do not eat up the oil fast enough, their creators stimulate the little bugs –

I sure hope the control doesn't eat the control because as Johnette says: "If we can't flit 'em, whatta we do?" But Johnette thought "... only God made bugs."

Bayou Microbe

ONE

The Mississippi reaches to the Gulf like a long brown arm that sifts land's pilfers through marshy fingers. And miles out in the Gulf's mist, the morning's wake-up call is the pot beating clatter of a helicopter trading roughnecks for the shift change.

The pilot hollers, "Hey you oil field

trash, better clean up your act! I'm bringing big-wigs out next trip out."

Then his craft, spewing brine wind is lost like a mosquito in the sun.

The early Gulf sun gets hot fast and schools of coastal fishermen out since before dawn head back into the marshland where night animals are turning in for Another day.

Deep in the bayou, the sun's rays spot the water line stained on the gray door of the cabin.

"Arr ...mand! Com ere and look at this plastic bucket!"

Armand meanders toward the sound of his wife's voice, his attention half on the pitted creosote pilings that support his cypress home on Bayou Perdu near the mouth of the mighty Mississippi where it dumps into the Gulf of Mexico.

"What is it?"

Celeste points at him with a chewed up plastic dish pan that had been lying by the back door. Shaking the remains at Armand she hollers, "Look what that damn mangy Catahoula mutt did!"

"Didn't. I tied him to that old pirogue leaning over there last night. Less he done drug it clean over here and then back he didn't eat not'n."

Armand laughs to his appreciative self, muttering how funny it was the thought of his old dog dragging the broken pirogue over so he could chew up the dishpan.

"But Armand look at this bucket!"

"I don't know what happen to that damn bucket I got to think about those rotten pilings. Dog don't eat plastic buckets there's not even any plastic left. Dogs chew up plastic. Leave a mess there's no mess."

Armand heads back around the side of the house grumbling to his self, "Never heard of no rotted creosote neither."

Celeste swishes back through the screen door slamming it behind her, "Mon Dieu! Can't have not'n. Can't have a damn thing!   Every damn thing I get gets torn up! Wouldn't be so funny if it were his damn fishing stuff."

Armand and Celeste, both born of misplaced Acadians that past migrated from Nova Scotia and settled South Louisiana, live on Bayou Perdu. Their French Acadian ancestry donned them Cajuns. They grew up together, married when they turned 15 and have lived all their lives near the mouth of the Mississippi where one can view the scattered oil rigs out in the Gulf's teal water. And when the inevitable hurricanes batter the coast, the deafening clatter of PHI helicopters flying EVAC, dance the glued-together-Crucifix that hangs crookedly over the door — Celeste long given up the chore of straightening it.

"Armand!" Celeste hollers back through the door before he got too far away. "You want heads off these squirrels in the jambalaya?"

Armand responds as if talking to the heavens, "You know Jacques Mayer and Johnettes they coming for to play Bouré. Jacques Mayer, he always want brains in his jambalaya."

TWO

Piquant sautéing garlic and onions permeated the heavy damp air when Armand opened the door to the sound of Jacques Mayer's lusty baritone invading the marsh with a slow mournful Cajun ballad lamenting the loss of his love.

"C'est le ça - pot que ma belle m'a don - né..."

"Bonjour Jacques Mayer, Johnette." Armand calls to his arriving guests.

"Comment ça va?"

"Comme ci, comme ça." Jacques Mayer laughingly gestures with an okay toss of his hand. "Et vous?"

"Très bien. Très bien." Armand responds.

Jacques Mayer, like Armand has a dark heavy Cajun look, coarse from hours in the sun making a living off the bayou. He stands a little more than a half foot taller than his wife Johnette's five feet — if she stretches a bit.

His primal nature and tight muscular shoulders are typical of the breed of men that work the crawfish nets while navigating a pirogue through the swampy bayous.

When Jacques Mayer entered the room, he warmed it with his essence and he went naturally to Celeste, who was already taking a beer from the ice box to hand to him.   With courtly Cajun flourish, he took the beer and hugged her at the same time.

"Ah ché, a perfect woman you are. If you ever want to rid of that burley husband I wait for you."

"So what do we do with your wife?"

"Ah Ché, I could use two good women."

Johnette laughs at Jacques Mayer's teasing and goes to the icebox to get herself a beer, then she lifts the lid of the heavy iron pot and tastes with her fingers the browned rice thick with onions, garlic, cayenne, basil, and parsley.

"Squirrel jambalaya? You make this for Jacques Mayer? C'est bon."

Jacques Mayer and Armand sat at the heavy wooden table and waited for Celeste and Johnette to bring their supper and the wives load and deliver plates of steamy browned rice laden heavy with dark chunks of squirrel along with tall glasses of sweetened iced tea. Bringing with her a spoon, Johnette hands it to Jacques Mayer for to crack the heads and suck out the squirrel brains. Amid fetching for and serving the men, Celeste and Johnette join in the meal and joshing conversation and afterwards without a word, rise to clear the table to ready for their customary game of Bouré.

It was a usual balmy night and the lyrical banter of Cajun French and the ante of copper pennies bouncing on the table, as they played, echoed throughout the cypress rooms. Each player was adept at rapidly shuffling, dealing, and retrieving won tricks while manipulating the changing trump card.

Bouré, or Cajun Bridge as it is commonly known, is learned early from their parents who learned it from their parents and the play is spontaneous and reflexive making conversation a potpourri.

"Hey Celeste you win one more trick and you can buy a new dish pan," teased Armand.

"That damn mangy Catahoula mutt chew up anything else and you'll need a trick to buy a new dog."

"It's not a mutt and I'm telling you for the last damn time my Catahoula Cur did not chew up your damn dish pan!

"Know-it-all thinks dog done drug that old broken pirogue over and chewed up that damn bucket. Quit bad mouthing my dog. He didn't chew nothing!"

"Did."

Armand's tuned ear heard the rasping bark of the Catahoula and trumping Celeste's trick, he rose to investigate.

"That damn mangy Catahoula mutt,"

griped Celeste, blaming her loss on the dog.

"'S not a mutt,'s a cur," Armand mutters, opening the door.

"Chewed up my bucket."

"Didn't."

Armand heads out into the yard, fanning back the barrage of mosquitoes that gathered round the yellow porch light and hollers at the dog to quiet down.

Amand mutters, "Dog must be getting old barking at the shadows."

But as he starts back up the porch steps, a lone figure moves into the light and Armand squinting into the shadows greets him, "Hey Sawyer! What you doing out this time of night? Come on in the house."

Celeste dumps the rest of her hand on the table and moves her chair to make room.

She whispers to Johnette, "Oh Johnette. How's my hair look? He's the picture man. Yellow hair. He so good looking make you want to slap your Grandma. Takes pictures of all the egrets and pelicans in the swamp. He give me one." She points to the large framed photograph of a brown pelican, emerging out of the brackish waters of the marsh carrying a speckled trout clenched in his bill. Snowy egrets salted the scene of Spanish moss flocked cypress trees.

The print, juxtaposed in primitive presentation, was suitable in content, yet in finesse, contradicted its surroundings.

Armand made the round of introductions, and Jacques Mayer extended his hand in welcome and Johnette stared openly childlike at Jacques Mayer and Sawyer, mesmerized by their oil and water contrast.

Celeste offers, "You come sit here," she tells Sawyer, patting the seat of the straight back-wooden chair next to her. "A beer, yes?"

Sawyer, as incongruous in this place as was his art, sat easy on the chair.

"I would much rather have coffee," he replied knowing that always, the stained white French coffee pot stay heated in a pan of water on the stove. A once white now brown sock hugged the slender drip section that filtered slowly fed boiling water.

Celeste hurries about, noticeably aware of herself, as she makes the tanned Nordic stranger welcome.

"I make a fresh pot," she offers.

"No. No, I like it just the way it is."

Sawyer had long acquired a liking for the rich black chicory laden coffee that was made by slowly dripping boiling water through fine grounds of dark roasted beans. He watched the coffee as Celeste poured the customary half cup into a milk glass cup now multicolored white mocha, as was the white porcelain drip pot. She slid in the chair beside him, flirting moving the cup to sit directly in front of him. He smiled self-consciously and leaned forward to inhale the aromatic steeping vapors. She was smitten with him. He knew it, but was uncertain of what she wanted and what to do about what she wanted.

When she talked to him, she looked at Armand first and Armand would ignore her. When Armand talked to him, Armand looked at Celeste first, and she would toss her head playfully smiling at Sawyer, then glance up for Armand's reaction. Sawyer looked at Armand for guidance, but when he spoke to either of them, Armand and Celeste just looked at each other.

Glancing frequently at Celeste, Armand tells Johnette and Jacques Mayer that Sawyer is a famous photographer that spends all his time in the bayou taking pictures. "Real famous," he explains. "Even written about in the *Times Picayune*." Armand diligently read his stack of New Orleans newspapers brought weekly by Sawyer.

THREE

"What it is you're doing? You take pictures at night, huh?" asks Jacques Mayer.

"No, I'm working myself back from Barataria Pass. One of the drilling company's storage facilities split and dumped 50,000 gallons of oil into the water. I wanted to see the damage first hand. Especially since the talk is, those oil-eating microbes are getting out of hand. And it seems there's another more serious leak at the LOOP no one will talk about, plus two strings of barges collided near Wax Lake.

More oil. That's a lot of destruction. And with those other spills over in Texas, moving this way, at this rate, I'm afraid there won't be any wildlife in the Gulf left for me to photograph. In Texas alone, there's been at least 4,000 spills since '73 and maybe 12 major spills within the past 14 years."

Johnette, hanging on his every word, asks, "What's eating microbes?"

Sawyer smiles at Johnette, uneasy with the attention, "They are very tiny bugs that have been developed to *eat* the chemicals that are accidentally spilled."

"If they got bugs, why not just flit em?" She was spellbound by his easy forceful voice and his compelling blue eyes, and to Celeste's aggravation Johnette would not stop staring at him.

Sawyer leans the chair back, locks his hands behind his head and tries not to smile, he stared for a moment at the ceiling composing his answer. "It isn't that easy. These bugs, microbes, were deliberately put out there, on the chemicals, oil, creosote, styrene, to get rid of them. Supposedly, the only thing that kills the bugs after they are unleashed is starvation."

Johnette's face turns red. She's unsure but nods like she understands.

"You know, Johnette," As Jacques Mayer speaks; subtly he puts his arm around her and gently reassures her. "We heard about em, they make over't the college. Armand read about it in the *Times Picayune*."

"Make em over't LSU? For sure?" Johnette asked.

Sawyer added, "It's a process called bioremediation to clean up chemical spills. They call them *Tiger Bugs* at LSU."

"I saw the men from Ella Shoe."
Celeste pipes in.

"From where? Ella huh?" Sawyer was puzzled.

Celeste articulates, "*L S U*, they were looking at my stuff."

"What stuff?"

"Used to be." She gives Armand a see what I told you look. "My pretty PVC patio set. Before that damn mangy Catahoula mutt chewed off the leg."

"Didn't." Armand quickly retaliates and adds, "And you ain't even got a patio. How'd you know they were from L S U ?" Armand mocks her articulation, rolling his L. He was teed off at the attention she was giving Sawyer.

"The brief case had a big purple and gold L, and a big purple and gold S, and a big purple and gold U on it and I know I don't have a patio but I enjoy to sit by the bayou. For your information, there were three men. And I saw all their brief cases.

"The man with the black glasses had the big purple and gold L S U and one said EPA and one said LOOP and I saw them clear as day."

"That's the LOOP, Louisiana Offshore Oil Platform," Armand interrupts her again.

She cast him an annoyed look and looked at Sawyer, "One had EPA. What's EPA?"

"That's the Environmental Protection Agency,"
replied Sawyer. "The watchdogs. But seems like in this case they're damned if they do and damned if they don't."

"Whyn't you ask em what they wanted?" Armand gave her a look.

"I had my hands in sticky flour and you don't like ruint biscuits. By the time I got to, they was gone and I forgot it."

"Your PVC furniture was chewed up." Sawyer edged up in his chair, as he comprehended what she had said.

"Uh huh."

"PVC, polyvinyl chloride, all petroleum based, made with oil," he mumbles."

FOUR

"Jee'sus." He had their undivided attention. Looking soberly around the table, he said, "This may be bigger than we figured. These bugs, microbes are microorganisms that eat virtually anything made from oil. And there are hundreds of different microorganisms. They're made by a process called bioremediation."

"Bio -reme...?" Armand starts.

"Bioremediation. It's..." Sawyer

seemingly exasperated pauses with a deep sigh.

"They make bugs?" Johnette asked. "I guess I'm out to lunch. I thought God made bugs."

"It's a bacteria. Bioremediation is the technology that uses these microbes, these oil-eating bugs, this devil created bacteria to eat virtually anything. It's like.

Well basically the bugs reduce the oil to fatty acids that will eventually sink and be eaten by marine life. They're really made to clean up hazardous waste and eat up pollution. But I'm really afraid that isn't all they are gonna eat.

"Bioremediation got its big break when Valdez spilled all that oil in Prince William Sound. Those bugs ate 74 miles of oil-smeared shoreline. Then, over near Galveston, a Norwegian tanker caught fire and ruptured. Lost three million gallons of light crude in the Gulf.

"They used foam, skimmers, booms and even set fire to it. You should have seen what it did to the shoreline. Tar balls, dead birds, dead fish. Then, they decided to feed the bugs." Sawyer pauses to a room of complete silence.

Johnette finally whispers, "If we can't flit 'em, whatta we do?"

"Well, Sawyer takes a deep breath almost smiling; they're supposed to just starve after the oil is gone. But, there seems to be a little something the boys didn't plan on. When the microbes didn't eat fast enough, or as fast as they wanted them to, the bug handlers developed chemicals called inducers. To stimulate their appetites. Now, we have some damn hungry little bugs.   "It looks like the bugs got bored eating just waste. When the oil spills and contaminants reach a low level, they switched to another food supply.

"Now, I don't know Johnette. I don't know what we can do. But I'm here to tell you. I saw it. Globs of oil. Tar balls. The black shoreline. Tentacles of reddish brown oil wrapping grabbing every living thing in sight. It stayed in blobs didn't break up. Streamers were 100 yards long. Dead crabs and mussels, blacken marine animals on shore.

"Cleanup crews vacuumed up heavy sludge that drifted, but the wind pushed a slick into the marshes. Talk about a sensitive place. It got into the marshland. The marshland is a living organic system. It is absolutely the most sensitive place it can be. Now the bugs are outside the perimeter and we have a backlash, a plethora of microbes, a deluge. This overkill could very well destroy a swamp."

Again, they sat in silence, each picturing their life without the marshland.

Sawyer was the first to speak, "I guess I ruined your party. Sorry but..."

Celeste scraped back her chair and jumps up. "It's all right. I can't concentrate with Uncle Earl barking every second." She slung open the door and hollers,   "You damn mangy Catahoula mutt. Shuuuut up!" She had forgotten her demure facade and realized it. Sheepishly she turns and grins at Sawyer then sashays back across the room.

"Uncle Earl's no mutt. ' S a cur," Armand snaps.

"Uncle Earl chewed my bucket!"

"Didn't!"

Sawyer smiled at the two of them, understanding their playfulness. He asked,

"Your dog's name is Uncle Earl?"

Everyone sat easy, happy to be off the bugs.

"Yep. He's a direct descendant of Governor Earl Long's dogs. The Catahoula. Louisiana's official state dog, he is. Uncle Earl's a Catahoula leopard dog cause his Pa was leopard but the Ma was spot. But they all have the *glass eye.*"

"Your dog has a glass eye?"

Jacques Mayer explained, his smile at Johnette telling her see everyone makes a mistake, saying he had been raising Catahoulas all his life like his father before him "They got light colored eyes, blue or amber or pale green. Mostly they got one eye 's brownish and one eye 's blue. The eyes, they haunt you. They bore right through you. Look like glass."

"Right," adds Armand.   "And they got webbed feet.

They say these dogs evolved to the swamp so to run in the mud.   But they don't track a ground spoor, they sniff the air when they run.   And yeah, they silent mouth hunter.   Hounds make a ruckus. Not Catahoulas, just steady lope along quiet like."

"Damn dog barks all the time," injects Celeste.

"Don't less som'em mess around," Armand directed to Celeste.

"I thought that silent tracking was just a characteristic of wild animals?" Sawyer asked, running his hands through his thick blonde hair, his thoughts ricocheting from bugs to dogs, dogs to bugs.

"Yep. Is. The Catahoula. He come from a red wolf." Armand told him. He was proud of Uncle Earl.   "Can trap a wild pig.   Takes a good dog to get a boar. Nothing worse than a male wood hog.

They'll slash you to bits.   Catahoula won't back off from anything.   And that damn dog'll tree a bobcat.   Yeah, they 'hot nose dogs'.   Won't follow a cold trail.   And not so big.   Bout 50 pounds.   People all over want these dogs.   Even that actor, name Carradine, come to Louisiana just to buy a Catahoula.   Tell you for sure, I don't know why he's barking so much. Usually dog just gets rowdy when somebody's messing around and takes up for his master.   He even protect Celeste, and she don't even like 'im."

"Do. I'm just mad because he chewed up my bucket."

"Didn't"

"Maybe he's barking at a Rougarou," Johnette suggests.

"A Rougarou?" Sawyer looks at

Johnette and she blushes.

"A Rougarou," she almost whispers, " 's werewolf that live in the bayou. My Paw Paw told me. The Rougarou is big and white, like a dog with a red tongue and red eyes that glow. If the Rougarou stop you, can't tell anybody for one year or you'll turn into one. Maybe Uncle Earl turn into the Rougarou. Jacques Mayer, I'm scared. Let's go home."

Jacques Mayer came around the table and pulled out Johnette's chair. He nuzzles his bearded chin against her neck, "I'm the only Rougarou that's gonna get you. Hey Sawyer you wanta go with us up the bayou as far as the Pointe."

"Sounds good to me," Sawyer replied.

Uncle Earl was stretched out near the bank of the bayou by the old broken pirogue watching his master watch him. His clear eyes reflected the yellow porch light and his spiny blue-gray mottled body begged for a rub. Sawyer, stepping over an armadillo that scurried back into the night, went to oblige the Catahoula. The swamp was calm, unusually quiet, and the familiar night clatter of deep pitched frog croon and cricket's squeal had stopped. The smell of bog must was thick in the night. You could touch the moisture in the air.

Armand heading back up the steps yelled back to his guests, "Hey all y'all! Jacques Mayer, Johnette, Sawyer come back on the weekend. We'll boil some crawfish. Jacques Mayer bring some corn. We'll pass a good time. Bon Soir."

"Armand, you want I should lock this door so the bugs or the Rougarou won't get in," Celeste closes the big cypress door behind Armand

and coquetry smiles at him.

"Don't give a damn."

"What'n hells wrong with you now?"

"Mon dieu woman.   You act like a New Orleans throw-ya sashaying around in front of Sawyer like that.

I'm going to bed."

Celeste just smiled bigger.   Oh tonight's gonna be good. 'S always good when Armand get jealous.   Umm mm huh tonight's gonna be good.

She hurries to finish the kitchen clean up and ready for bed.

FIVE

The aloe vera's morning drink dripped down the sill, gleaming the morning sun that filtered into the kitchen window through Spanish moss draped like Christmas tinsel over tree limbs. The yellow light diffracted through Celeste's transparent house dress, silhouetting her stocky thighs. Armand watches her making breakfast thinking, that, and the smell of frying bacon and dripped coffee was as good as it gets.

"Celeste, Listen to what it says in this newspaper.   It says here that Governor Edwards been called to approve the use of those oil-eating microbes in the marshland."

"Like Sawyer said?"

"Like   it   says   here,   "Armand emphasized.

"That   there   was   an   oil   spill   at Barataria Pass and another one because of a broken underground pipeline. It says the sheen worked into a swamp south of the navigation canal and into the coastal marsh and this is where the booms and skimmer won't work. There's trouble from Glenco to Little Lake to Buras across the Gulf."

"When it happen?"

"This paper was on the stack Sawyer brought last time. Last week. Says the Coast Guard has a ban on fishing and they closed oyster beds. Let me just read the rest.

This   slick   caused   major
environmental damage,"

Amands reads on:

*"The   Intracoastal   Waterway   is
closed   with   vessels   backed   up
traveling slowly at 1 knot instead of 5
or 6 knots in order to avoid wakes that
would stir up the slick. Cleanup crews
continue to remove the toxic material
from the area.   Vacuum barges and
skimmer vessels are operating picking
up remnants of the spill.   Coast Guard
warns   that   travel   is   dangerous
because of current.*

"

MAJOR TEXAS SPILL

A 500,000 gallon spill from a sinking barge in the Houston Ship Channel was reported today. This major spill compounded the damage of an earlier spill from a barge tanker collision.

" The Greek tanker Shinoussa collided with two barges under tow dumping 315 gallons of refinery oil into the Channel.

" While both spills are under investigation, the Federal State Response Team spread 100 pounds of oil-eating bacteria around Houston Point and its marshes in an attempt to forestall major environmental damage."

The knock on the door startled both of them. Armand stands to watch as Celeste moved toward the door wiping her hands on her housedress.

A tall, rather nervous, man wearing a damp gray suit stood outside the screen door. Next to him stood another man, shorter, casually dressed, fidgeting about.

The tall man spoke, "Good morning Ma'am. Is your husband home.? "

Celeste, never speaking, steps aside and looks to
Armand who was already heading for the door looking past them toward the landing, wondering why he had not heard them come up.

"Good morning sir. My name is Hal Koch. Could I have a word with you this morning?" The tall man said.

"Armand LeDay. How you doing? " Armand was guarded but he invited, "Come on in. Seat yourself."   He points to the long wooden table.

Still standing, Koch places his brief case on the table and starts, "I'm with the SEC Oil Refinery. We're based over in Cameron."

"You don't sound like you're from Cameron," Armand interrupts him.

"Well, actually I'm from New Jersey, where we have our corporate offices. But I assure you our oil fields are based out of Cameron. This is Jud Mentz. He's with the Environmental Protection Agency."   He hands Armand a business card.

Celeste poured two more cups of coffee and sat them before the two men, sitting explicitly out of place, at her table, they murmured their thanks. She doesn't speak a word, just pulls up a chair beside Armand, and stares at the little man on a horse sewn on Jud Mentz's knit shirt. Koch looked damp in his gray business suit.

"Sure is a great place you got here," Koch starts in an attempt to be friendly.

"What y'all doing out here?" Armand scratches his yet unshaven chin.

"I guess I'll get right to the point. Mr. LeDay, we're expanding our operations in the marshland. We've already made arrangements with all your neighbors to purchase their land ..."

"Neighbors?" Armand stopped him. "What neighbors?"

"Well, I mean, property owners, as close as they get. We are in the market for land from Bayou Perdu back down to the Gulf of Mexico."

"Already decided. Not for sale." Armand was adamant.

"Mr. LeDay. As I was saying, before

you decide, we are prepared to offer you quite a lucrative price for this land."

"Lucrative?" Celeste found her voice.

"Yes Ma'am. I'm authorized by SEC to offer you as much as $50,000 for the land and the buildings on it." Koch smiles at Celeste giving her his best shot.

Armand laughs lightly and says, "Yeah."

Koch ignores Armand's laugh and adds, "In addition, Mr. LeDay, we'll give you a brand new aluminum bateau and motor."

"What for?" Celeste watches Armand laugh.

"Well Ma'am..."

"I'm Mrs. LeDay."

"Yes Ma'am. Mrs. LeDay, you can use the bateau is for whatever you want."

"I know what a damn bateau is for.

For what for you want the land?" She looks cleverly at Armand whose laugh turned in to a smile.

"As I explained before," he patronizing patiently smiled at Celeste, "we're expanding our operations." To Armand he adds, "Mr. LeDay, I am prepared to increase my offer to $65,000 but I'm afraid that's as high as I can go."

Armand started laughing so hard that he started coughing.

Koch was notably at a disadvantage, confused at Armand's amusement to his proposal, so he stood as to leave. Jud Mentz, who had not said a word, followed suit. Koch heads for the door and said, "Look why don't you both think about it and we'll come back in a few days to discuss it with you again."

Armand half-heartedly apologizes as he let them out the door, but he and Celeste were laughing so hard they put their arms around each other and tears streamed down their faces.

"Yeah, Celeste, Jacques Mayer, he playing a good one. This land's not worth more'n $5,000. Think I'd fall for that."

Later Celeste, cleaning the table picks up the business card left there.

"Armand, this card look real. See, it says *Hal E. Koch SEC Oil Refinery, INC.* and the letters are raised up and gold. Anyhow that man, he talks funny. New Jersey? Sounds like a foreigner or something. What you think?"

"I think Jacques Mayer's funning. $65,000 and a new bateau? Hmm? Crazy. Lotta money for this land? But we'll find out when he comes for the crawfish boil Saturday."

SIX

As the day broke, the muggy Saturday morning air seeped fast through seines of tangled gray moss dangling on swamp-bred trees. Leaving a balmy dirt smell, the strained sun heated the earth fast as Armand poled his pirogue back through the marsh. He had gotten up early to run the crawfish nets and collect the live catch for the day's festivity. The season was early and the catch was good because the crawfish were hungry for the chunks of melt that Armand had dropped into the traps.

He had set out the day before, in the shallow lakes of the marsh the round mesh traps, and dropped into the bottom of them the shad and animal fat bait that brought in the hundreds of hungry crawfish that once crawled in the traps could not get out.

Skillfully Armand sided up to the landing in front of his home on the bayou where the day's festivity was already in full swing. Ignoring Armand's call for help from the landing, Celeste, cursing Uncle Earl, propped up the missing table leg. Jacques Mayer smiling at Celeste's snub headed down to help Armand. He, along with Johnette and half a dozen others, had arrived early
to help with preparations.

Ignoring the live mudbug claws that tickled their backs, Armand and Jacques Mayer swung cross their brawny shoulders the heavy sacks of live crawfish and carried them to a washtub of salty water next to where Jacques Mayer had started a large pot of water to boil over the iron gas boiler.

Johnette and Celeste halved lemons and sorted small red potatoes and corn to add to the boiling water along with the cayenne, garlic, lemons, and liquid hot seasonings. Tubs of iced beer had been placed around the table where Johnette had dropped a load of newspapers to cover the table.

Armand dumped a sack of the live crawfish in the salty water and then, all at once, poured several more boxes of salt atop of them to make the crawfish spit out the mud.

Once they were purged, he and Jacques Mayer grabbed both sides of the large strainer that sat inside the tub, and drained off the salt water. They lowered the strainer of crawfish slowly into the boiling seasoned water. And like they had done so many times before, ceremonially, after adding the vegetables that Celeste had prepared, they opened a beer to sit and watch the pot boil. It didn't take long before Armand cut the fire to let the crawfish set to soak up the seasoning.

This was his time to purge another sack of crawfish and then greet his guests.

The steamy rich smell of the tangy hot delicacy hung low in the air and just about all the company had arrived. A crowd of around 20 mulled about and everyone talked, teased and laughed at the same time. Armand shook hands with the men and kissed the women. And yelled at the children for teasing Uncle Earl. Armand's cousins, Merle and Earl, set up on the steps to play their gregarious Cajun music and when Merle hit the first few notes of *Jolie Blonde* on his fiddle and was joined by Earl's charismatic twang on his squeezebox, the rapid beat of Cajun swamp rock rang down the canal. The brusque beat of the first few notes drew couples to dance on the rolled out sheet of

linoleum that Armand kept by the pilings for such an

occasion.   Celeste   danced   among   the dancers that skillfully swayed and turned in perfect   rhythm   to   the   Cajun   two-step, dancing the same steps to the same music that their parents had danced to in the past.

The children kept to the edge of the makeshift dance floor dancing in unison around the yard, imitating their parents.

Armand, tapping his foot with the beat, jumped up from his post to join

Celeste on the dance floor. He grabbed her round her waist, taunting, "Come here woman. I teach you how to do this dance." And they two-stepped round the yard in perfect unison, swaying and turning catching every beat of the rollicking music. He kisses her and leaves her as the song ends to return to his post just in time to help Jacques Mayer lift the heavy strainer of crawfish.

As they poured the boiled crawfish and spicy vegetables in the middle of spread out newspapers on the table, the pungent eruption of steam drew everyone to the tables. Everyone grabs a beer and pulls up a chair. With ease, adults and children alike pulled off the meaty crawdad tails and then sucked the juice from the head. With learned cadence they threw the spent heads in a pile and crushed with their fingers the tail for ease in peeling the first

strip of hard shell so they pull out the meat out with their teeth. The prattle and laughter and spent heads pile up fast, and as fast as
they piled the men dumped them back into the bayou 'to feed the catfish', then waited for the next pot to season just right. The music makers took time off to eat and as always Armand and Jacques, who did the cooking ate last, claiming the last boil to be the best yet, Armand rescuing one live crawfish to put atop the heap vowing to the amazed kids that only one lived.

Later in the evening, after Celeste had pulled off the heads and cleaned the fat from the left over crawfish, to save and make étouffée, Armand told her that he had talked to Jacques Mayer and Jacques claimed that he had nothing to do with that Koch man coming by.

"I guess he telling the truth," Celeste replied. "I heard Ethel Thibodeaux telling, and she knows ever thing that is going on from the West Bank to Baton Rouge, that the Melancons over to Port Fouchon had sold out and she knew more that did too. Melancons already moved to New Orleans."

They didn't talk about it until the next day when they returned from the Christ King Church and Sunday morning mass.

Armand told Celeste, "Maybe this is for real, I don't know. Yeah 's real. Jacques Mayer didn't send them. What you think?"

Celeste didn't answer and all day long Armand and Celeste moped quietly around the house, each picturing what they would do if they left the bayou. Each spending $65,000 in private dreams. Celeste even forgot to gripe about Uncle Earl. It was evening before they spoke of it again.

"Armand, You ever thought of living in Baton Rouge?"

"No Celeste. I don't want to live in a great big city."

"What you know about Baton Rouge?" asked Celeste "Your governor, Edwin Edwards, lives in Baton Rouge."

"Well, last year when I went over to Sorrento and then over the Sunshine Bridge to Baton Rouge and it's too big. You think just because you live in Baton Rouge you get invited to dinner with Gove'nor Edwards?"

Celeste looked at him for a long moment and then said, "Sorrento's good."

SEVEN

The knock on the door came early. Armand got up and answered the door himself. He was grave. Koch came alone.

"Good morning Mr. LeDay.   Mrs. LeDay."

"How you doing?"

"Sorry to come so early but my company has authorized me to make you a final offer.   I'm afraid you have us at a serious disadvantage." He spoke hurriedly looking back and forth between Celeste and Armand guardedly as if he needed to get it

all said before Armand laughed again.
"It's a lot more than any of your neighbors, or rather other property owners in the area — more than we gave them. Time is of the essence ..."

"Why you talk like that? Celeste interrupts.

"Like what?"

Armand frowns at Celeste. "Nothing, sorry." She mumbled.

"This lands worth..." Armand starts.

"SEC Oil Company has authorized me to make you a final offer of $125,000 and that's a lot more than any other property owner in the area has gotten."

Celeste recovers first from the shock of the tremendous offer. "What for you give us more?"

"Mrs. LeDay, I just don't have time to

dicker. I must get my operations under way. The pressure is great. We need this land. This is for everything. Everything. Even personal belongings. Furniture, everything."

"When you want it?" Armand had made up his mind.

"Yesterday." Koch hurriedly replied. But when Armand gave him an impatient look he added, "Today. I mean as soon as possible."

"Today? We gotta pack." Armand absently replies.

"No Mr. LeDay. You don't understand." Koch tells him nervously.

"We're buying everything. Everything except what you're wearing."

"I gotta take my Jesus?" Celeste points to the crooked plastic Crucifix hanging over the door..

Koch stares at the plastic fixture for a few moments and says, "Sorry Ma'am. I mean EVERYTHING."

"You can have that old PVC patio set that damn mangy Catahoula mutt chewed up."

"Didn't"

"Mrs. LeDay, you can buy yourself a new patio set."

Armand asks, "And a new bateau with a 50 Evinrude. Right?"

"Right." Koch stood and offered his hand, "We have a deal."

"Deal." Armand shook his hand, passing a cold chill between them.

Armand and Celeste just sat for a while thinking before Celeste spoke, "Armand, I'm scared but I'm gonna pack."

Armand stopped her and put his arms around her, "Celeste, I'll buy you one of those condominiums and first thing we'll have a cochon de lait and invite Jacques Mayer and Johnette and this time I'll 'buy' you one of Sawyer's pictures. We'll have beignets ever morning and cafe au lait to pass it down. Anyway the bayou 's not the same. Copters flying over all the time. Can't even hear a bull frog sometimes."

"Okay Armand Okay." Celeste went into the bedroom to look around.. She stared at the pink plastic crucifix hanging on the bedroom wall and tugged nervously at the floral cotton skirt of her house dress. Then she took the pink plastic crucifix off the wall and passed her hand over the darker cross imprint on the cypress board. She stuck it in her pocket and later hid it on the porch in the bag that Koch said they could take with them.

It was late evening on the bayou and early dampness had begun to set in. The cricket squeal started and stopped when two boats pulled up to the landing. Koch drove a brand new dark green 16-foot aluminum bateau with a brand new 50 Evinrude. It was completely rigged with a trolling motor, gauges, seats. A dream come true and Armand couldn't take his eyes off the rig.

"I don't mean to rush you but we need to get going here." Koch and the man in the other boat were hurriedly unloading large metal cans and wooden boxes that were marked each with a large black diamond that had a number in the center.

"Sure. I'll get Celeste. Get in Uncle Earl."

This was *his* boat now.

Armand walked slowly the path back up to the steps leading to the cypress porch, a million family memories passing by; he stopped and absently looked at eaten away creosote pilings.

Some damn strong termites he thinks. "Come on Celeste. I'm gonna catch some specs in that bateau. Sure is fine!"

EIGHT

Armand drove his new bateau slowly up the middle of the bayou. Dark green wakes pushed out easy from the slow moving boat sloshing against blacken mossy cypress stumps and grassy banks. Green black bubble gator eyes peeked at them from just above water's surface. Uncle Earl sat tall watching for early coons moving in the dim light.

"Armand, what that noise?"

"Just more of those damn copters."

"No Armand. Listen?"

"Wanna go back and see?"

"No Armand.   Très gris gris to go back. No."

Armand stopped the motor and looked back toward the old family home. There were plumes of dirty brindle smoke billowing from reddish brown flames.

At once, a deluge of helicopters came fast over them, then were lost from sight in a black cloud against a gray sky. The cloud took over the heavens.

Waves of unbleached cotton loomed upwards and the smell of burning creosote stung their nostrils. The outline of orange peaks pointed above the trees.

"Yeah," she whispers, "Très mal gris gris."

Celeste moved to the back of the boat and took the pink plastic crucifix from her bag. "Let's go Armand."

Celeste didn't look back again, she just held the crucifix tightly in her hand and above the noise of the Evinrude, she hollered, "Armand! Look at this crucifix! That damn mangy Catahoula mutt done chewed off the bottom the cross and part of Jesus' legs!"

"Didn't."

The End

...perhaps